W9-BGE-013

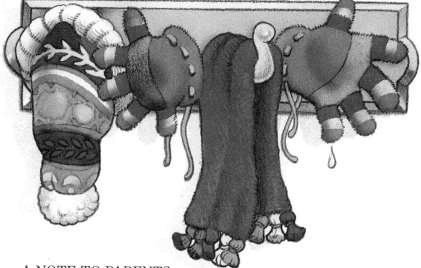

A NOTE TO PARENTS

Early Step into Reading Books are designed for preschoolers and kindergartners who are just getting ready to read. The words are easy, the type is big, and the stories are packed with rhyme, rhythm, and repetition.

We suggest that you read this book to your child the first few times, pointing to each word as you go. Soon your child will start saying the words with you. And before long, he or she will try to read the story alone. Don't be surprised if your child uses the pictures to figure out the text—that's what they're there for! The important thing is to develop your child's confidence—and to show your child that reading is fun.

When your child is ready to move on, try the rest of the steps in our Step into Reading series. **Step 1 Books** (preschool–grade 1) feature the same easy-to-read type as the Early Step into Reading Books, but with more words per page. **Step 2 Books** (grades 1–3) are both longer and slightly more difficult, while **Step 3 Books** (grades 2–3) introduce readers to paragraphs and fully developed plot lines. **Step 4 Books** (grades 2–4) offer exciting nonfiction for the increasingly independent reader.

The grade levels assigned to the five steps are intended only as guides. Some children move through all five steps very rapidly; others climb the steps over a period of several years. Either way, these books will help your child "step into reading" in style!

http://www.randomhouse.com/

Library of Congress Cataloging-in-Publication Data
Armstrong, Jennifer. The snowball / by Jennifer Armstrong ; illustrated by Jean Pidgeon.
    p. cm. — (Early step into reading)
SUMMARY: A snowball rolls down a hill, growing in size and picking up people and
objects as it goes.
ISBN 0-679-86444-X (pbk.) — ISBN 0-679-96444-4 (lib. bdg.)
[1. Snow—Fiction. 2. Stories in rhyme.] I. Pidgeon, Jean, ill. II. Title III. Series
PZ8.3.A63Sn 1996 94-48883 [E]—dc20

Printed in the United States of America   10 9 8

STEP INTO READING is a trademark of Random House, Inc.

Early Step into Reading™

THE
SNOWBALL

by Jennifer Armstrong
illustrated by Jean Pidgeon

Random House 🏠 New York

I saw a snowball
on a hill.

It rolled along
and picked up Bill!

It rolled along
with Bill inside.

It rolled along
and picked up Clyde.

What a ride!

I saw a snowball
with four feet.

It rolled along
and picked up Pete.

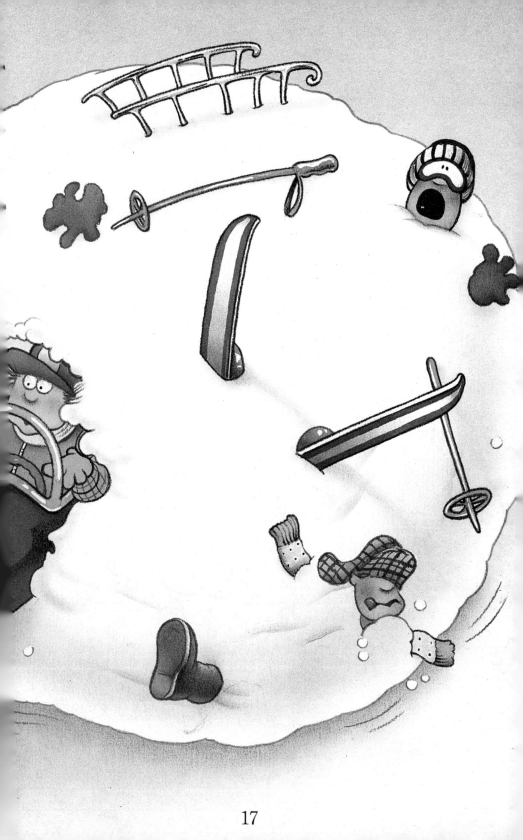

It rolled him up
as quick as that!

It rolled along
and picked up Pat.

AND her hat!

I saw a snowball
roll past Lee.

It rolled along
and picked up ME!

It rolled! It bounced!

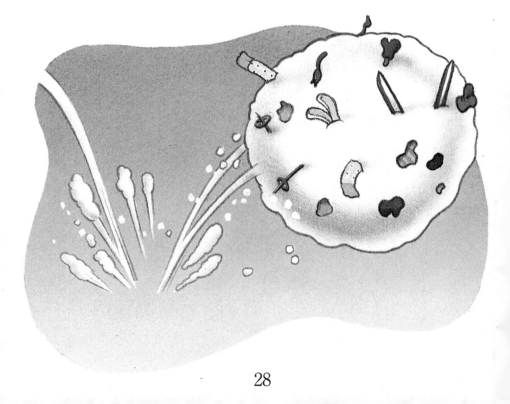

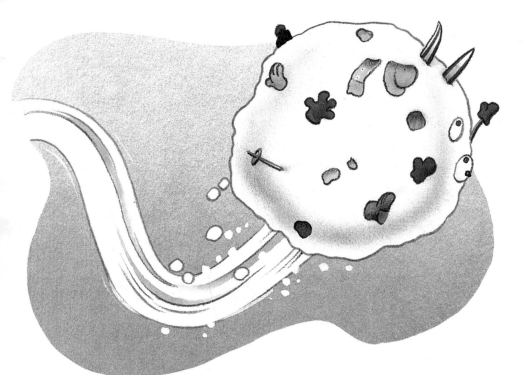

It dipped! It dashed!

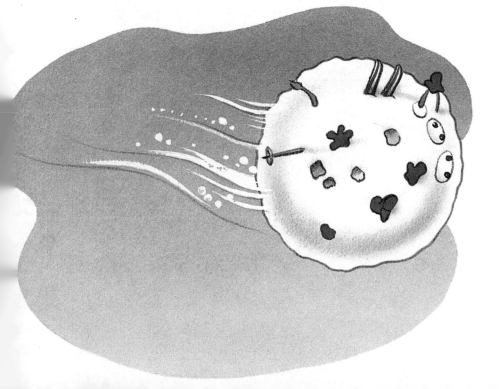

It rolled along
until it SMASHED!

THE END